Abomination in Wax
A Christmas Story
By
Judith Sonnet

12/12/2024

ISBN: 9798303438286

Independently Published

Edited by Danielle Yeager

Cover art: *St. Nicholas* by Robert Walter Weir. Smithsonian American Art Museum, Museum purchase

ca. 1837

Cover layout/design by Ruth Anna Evans

Abomination in Wax

❄ ❄ ❄

Clovehitch knocked on the massive wooden door. He stepped back and waited, tutting impatiently to himself. He didn't like the cold, and he liked the rain even less. The fact that the clouds couldn't decide whether they wanted to rain or snow vexed him endlessly.

Bloody awful night for this business. Awful night.

The door swung open with an operatic creak.

"Yes?" asked the answerer.

"You're Mr. Tinsel?" Clovehitch asked. He knew who the man was, but he wanted to make the old bastard uncomfortable.

"Yes," the wiry man said with an inscrutable expression. He seemed, to Clovehitch, as if he was unbothered by the presence of a late-night visitor.

"Mr. Partridge Tinsel? Owner and proprietor of this here establishment?"

"Aye. 'Tis I. It's a bit late for a tour, though."

Clovehitch almost laughed. "Trust me, Mr. Tinsel, I wouldn't be visiting your . . . business . . . if it wasn't important."

Above Clovehitch's head hung a banner, which read *MR. TINSEL'S NIGHTMARE WAX MUSEUM*. Clovehitch had been keeping a weary eye on the place since it'd opened in October. Everyone in town had been excited about the wax museum, but it was quickly decided that the exhibits were much too gruesome, and that it would behoove the good citizens of Downwhich to avoid the business entirely and hope it drained money and left.

That had been in October . . . now it was December, just about Christmas. Although Tinsel's patronage had plummeted, he seemed immovable.

Clovehitch—who'd been a constable since he was a lad—suspected he had regular customers. Morbid folks who came by the museum once or twice a week and kept the lights on for special tours. There were rumors going around that Tinsel had a special room that featured darker stuff than the horror he openly displayed for paying folk. This seedier room was off-limits, unless one was willing to spend an exorbitant fee. Of course, all of this was rumor fodder, but Clovehitch fancied himself as much a detective as he was a constable, so he kept his ear to the ground and listened when people spoke in whispers.

That said, no one had been whispering tonight. There'd been an uproar when Dooley came stumbling into the bar, mortified and ghostly. The old man had demanded a drink so loudly he'd stopped the band. He pounded his fist against the bar top and hollered, "Can ya hear me? I asked fer a drink and I need one! I jus' saw the corpse of my Molly!"

Molly Dooley had been butchered in the street. Clovehitch had seen her body as it was wrapped in a sheet and loaded into the back of an ambulance. He'd made sure her father had never taken a look at her body, even when he'd begged to.

"You don't wanna see that, Mr. Dooley," Clovehitch had said, a hand laid against the barrel chest of the weeping farmer.

Even hearing mention of Molly Dooley sent shiver-inducing memories into Clovehitch's head. He saw her laid out in the snow-drenched alley, all torn and tattered as if something with claws had attacked her. Her face had been shredded, exposing the yellowed bone beneath. Her guts had been pulled from her eviscerated abdomen to form a knotted circle around her. She looked like a human sacrifice on an altar composed of her own bloody fluids. There was not even a scrap of clothing to be found. The entirety of her secrets had been laid bare for all to see, so long as they had been brave enough to glance down the dark alley as they strolled past. The heat from her body had escaped her, so her flesh was turgid and glossy. The blood had crystalized and looked like a painting of spilled wine.

These images remained in Clovehitch's head, even though it had been going on five years since poor Molly Dooley had been butchered. Five years, and now . . . Eustace Dooley was talking about having seen her?

He must've been mad or already drunk.

Standing up from his corner, Clovehitch steadily approached the man while he wept into his beer. Dooley had lost weight and strength since his daughter had been murdered. The mother had died in childbirth, and Dooley had never remarried. He was a lonely man, surrendered to grief and heartache.

"Oh, Molly. Dear Molly!" Dooley sobbed.

Clovehitch—who was tall, dark, and bearded—placed a hand on the man's back. Dooley jittered and flinched, but relaxed when he saw it was an old friend taking his side.

"What's this talk?" Clovehitch asked.

The band was playing again. A real moody tune that sounded like it'd been dredged up from a battlefield. Clovehitch leaned in close so he could hear Dooley better.

The farmer whipped around and grabbed Clovehitch by the cuffs of his coat. He dragged the lawman close and breathed heavily into his mouth, as if Dooley was preparing to lay a kiss on Clovehitch's lips. The constable tried to buck away, but Dooley's grip was as firm as a constricting snake.

"You saw her! You saw my Molly! I didn't . . . not 'til tonight! But that's the thing of it, sir. I didn't *have* to see my sweet daughter's ravaged body. I pictured it! Every night, I dreamed new horrors that'd befallen her innocent flesh! And that . . . that *madman* knew what I dreamed and put it in wax!"

"You're not making sense!" Clovehitch expelled. "Come, then. Let's go to the station and get you sobered—"

"This is my first drink of the night, Clove! It ain't drink that's stirred me so! It's grief! I tell you . . . that monster, Minstrel . . . no . . . Tinsel! Yes, that's his name! He's a fiend, and you'd best heed my words on the matter!"

'What do you mean, Dooley?" Clovehitch rasped.

They had an audience. The patrons at the bar were pretending not to hear nor look, but they were doing both. Clovehitch wished he could drag Dooley away and continue this discussion in private.

Dooley whirled, holding his arms up for attention. "Citizens of Downwhich! Hear me! The man, Partridge Tinsel, is nothing more than a demon!"

A brave drunk honked with laughter.

A more sympathetic drunk leaned toward Dooley from his seat at the bar. "Yer wacked, Dooley. And anyone would be in yer shoes. What ya need is good rest and some calm. Here. Sit with me and share a drink. We can 'member the good times with Molly."

"Ain't right what done ta 'er," a slovenly drunk growled. "Like an animal. In the streets. Cold business, that. Cold and awful."

"Listen to me!" Dooley projected. "Listen! I'm not lying and I'm not mad! Tinsel . . . he's been pestering me for weeks now. He's written me letters cordially inviting me to test his latest exhibit before it was aired to the public! He said he wanted fresh eyes and an honest opinion. I thought he was bothersome at first, but I came around to the idea. As if he'd implanted it in my head!"

Dooley tapped a hard finger against his balding noggin. His eyes were popping from their sockets and froth clung to the sides of his chapped mouth.

Clovehitch wanted to take the man to the station, but he was off duty . . . and the performance was spectacular. In seconds, Dooley had calmed a rowdy bar and convinced all to hear his voice and his only.

"So's I decided to accept his offer. He gave me the time he wanted me, and I showed up not . . . two hours ago. I'd never been to his ghastly museum before, and he told me that's why he selected me. Because I'd know how new patrons felt after taking in a*ll* his horrors at once. I'll admit, I was feeling a mite nervous. After what happened to Molly, I can't much say I have a taste fer the macabre. He saw my jitters and soothed them, informing me that he was seeking to horrify but also to entertain. That if I ever got ta feelin' faint, all I need do was tug his arm and tell him I needed a break."

Like Dooley, Clovehitch had never before entered Tinsel's museum. It wasn't that he was frightened . . . he was repulsed by the concept. He'd heard from a young one that there were wax figures that had been beheaded by guillotine, that there'd been a witch tied to a stake, and half of her wax face had sloughed away to expose the skull beneath. Tinted red with caramelized gore!

Outside, the snow shifted and rain began to fall. It chittered on the ceiling of the tavern, adding a strange ambiance to Dooley's woeful tale.

❄ ❄ ❄

The story of the Wax Museum, as Dooley portrayed it when telling his tale at the tavern:

Dooley followed Tinsel into the museum. His nerves had been abated by the presence of the museum proprietor. Tinsel was such a harmless-looking fellow. Squat, spindly limbed, and whiskered. He reminded Dooley of an old grandpa, and his ridiculous dress made him comical. Tinsel was dressed like Jack the Ripper, with a dusty, night-black cowl, a top hat, and a black mask that obscured his eyes. The mask was askew and the hat tumbled off his scaly head when he walked too fast.

"When are you planning on unveiling this . . . new segment?" Dooley asked.

"Christmas," Tinsel said. "Like a new gift for the entire town to unwrap."

"Sure. Sure." Dooley held his thoughts in his chest. He didn't think the simple, Christian villagers of Downwhich would be too keen on coming to the wax museum on the holiest of holidays. Although, Dooley had once heard that Christmas had been a pagan holiday before the Christians laid claim to it.

But he was not a theological academic, and he knew very little of history. Dooley was an easygoing man, and he believed in God and considered that enough.

He was thankful the museum was warm. The streets outside were patched with snow and gurgling rain puddles. The wind was as bitter as a striking blade, and the clouds had turned a depressing gray. It made him feel as if he was staring at the outside world from inside a shaken snow globe.

He sometimes referred to the snow as

"Molly weather." He hated himself for trivializing the death of his only daughter like that, but it was what he considered a survival mechanism.

The lobby was quaint and small. There was a taxidermy deer and a pheasant in midflight. There was also a placard that warned people of the terrors they were about to observe within the confines of the museum.

"How's business?" Dooley asked with an awkward stance.

"Middling, but I make enough. Hopefully, this latest addition will convince the more stalwart crowd to step inside. Have you ever been to a wax museum before?"

"No. Can't say I've been to a *museum* before." Dooley shrugged. "You must think me uncultured."

"No," Tinsel said. "Just unexposed. Well, allow me to warn you . . . the figures are realistic. Almost lifelike. Quite different from store mannequins. You might even be convinced that some of them are made of flesh and dripping blood. They aren't. The process of wax sculpting is long and complicated. I build the models with my own hands and paint them too. It's all a farce, but you'll struggle to comprehend that once you lay your eyes on them. I'm not being hyperbolic. I'm telling you to be cautious." Tinsel peeled apart a red velvet curtain that led into the chambers of his museum.

The first thing Dooley noted when he walked through the threshold was the smell. The wax stench was pungent, as was the dust that had collected on the figures. He sneezed, apologized, and used a handkerchief to wipe his runny nose.

Dooley walked up to the first exhibit and took it in.

"My!" the farmer exclaimed.

The man was frozen, but Dooley wouldn't have been surprised if he suddenly leapt into vibrant action. He was so lifelike! Tinsel had even drawn veins, which appeared to thrum with blood beneath the surface of his epidermis.

The man was standing upright. From the neck down, he looked like an aristocrat. He wore a fancy floral suit and shiny shoes with bright buckles.

His own issue was the axe, which had been lodged into his skull. The blade split his head down the middle and rested between his eyes. The right one was hanging from its socket by a dangling, chunky nerve. The left had turned moon white, and gunky, bloodred tears streamed down his cheek.

“My!” Dooley repeated. ‘Who is this poor bastard?”

“Of my own invention. I haven’t given him a proper name, but if you’ll observe the plaque, it will give you the title of the piece!”

Dooley looked down at the plaque on a waist-high pulpit. It read *A Splitting Headache.*

“A little morbid humor,” Tinsel stated. “Gallows Humor. If we cannot laugh at the horrors of reality, I figure it’d drive us insane. Don’t you agree?”

Maybe, Dooley supposed, that was why he referred to the cold as “Molly weather.” He felt guilty all over again.

“What’s next?” Dooley asked, allowing

his tour guide to lead him.

"Another from my dark imagination. I call this one, *Caught in a Web*!"

The next piece was even more disturbing than the last, although it contained far less gore. Dooley stared with enraptured horror at the figure.

A woman was caught in a massive spiderweb that ensnared her arms and separated her legs. Her mouth was open in a mute scream, and her eyes were pinched shut. She was scantily clad, which further reddened Dooley's mortified face. Clutching her breast like a hairy palm was a giant eight-legged spider. Another was on her naked thigh, sinking its fangs into her pale flesh. Twin streams of blood dribbled down her leg and pooled below her hovering foot.

"Are you scared of spiders, Mr. Dooley?" Tinsel asked.

"Y-yes." Dooley admitted. "Let's move past this one!"

The wax artist barked with snide laughter, which unnerved poor Dooley. The two waddled away from the entrapped girl and toward the next installment.

In this one, a young boy was hanging by the neck from a greasy rope. His body spun in slow circles, giving Dooley a shot of the dead child from every angle. He couldn't have been more than eight years old. His face was purple, and his tongue was enlarged and jutting from his swollen mouth. Dooley saw, with revulsion, that the crotch of the boy's pants was permanently stained and glistening. Perpetually wet.

"What's the genesis of this 'un?" Dooley asked, although he was not quite sure he wanted to know the answer.

"This is the first of the museum that's based upon true events, good Dooley," Tinsel stated. "The lad you see here is young Emmet Dinker. He and his brother often played a cruel game with their neighbors. It was called 'Hangman.' They'd pick one member of their herd to be 'the criminal,' and the rest were 'townspeople.' What followed was a simple game of hide-and-go-seek . . . only, when the criminal was found, the townspeople would carry him up to the barn and they'd wrap a rope around him and drop him into a haymow. For poor Emmet, the game turned frighteningly real when he was dropped, and it was discovered that the rope had been tied to one of the beams in the loft. Rather than falling harmlessly into the hay, he dangled and died of strangulation!"

"How cruel!"

"Quite!"

"And none of the other boys thought to cut him down?"

"His brother testified that the sudden stopping of the rope and Emmet's squeals had terrified them. They scuttled down from the loft and scampered off!"

Dooley couldn't see Tinsel's eyes, but he imagined they'd gone misty and bewildered.

"They were too terrified by the prospect of his death . . . to even consider preventing it. And they didn't tell their parents. Emmet was discovered that night by his father, who'd gone into the barn to see if he'd fallen asleep there after he'd failed to come home for dinner and bedtime. His brother didn't admit to any wrongdoing until he heard tell that suicides didn't go to Heaven, and he didn't want anyone thinking his poor brother had committed such an act."

"What a miserable story! Almost can't believe it's true!"

"It is."

"And this is exactly what he looked like? All . . . purple faced?"

"Yes. I find embellishments to be crude. Reality is so much more sickening, don't you agree?"

Dooley had to.

They continued down the row of figures, taking in horrific sights. There were the Salem witches, the poisoned, stabbed, and drowned figure of Rasputin, and even the corpse of Franz Ferdinand! There was a body leaning against a guillotine, the blade already fallen and his bleeding head staring up from a basket.

Dooley got queasy when the two entered

a room dedicated to barbaric acts of medieval torture. There was a smell like raw meat in this room, and Dooley wondered if it was his imagination, or if Tinsel was keeping rotten meat beneath the floorboards to accentuate the nauseous horror of torture.

A frail man was pinned to a rack. A bear-sized brute was twisting a wheel, which tightened the ropes affixed to the victim's limbs. A small seam had torn open in the crying figure's left armpit. Blood decorated the wooden slat he lay upon.

"Oh, great God in Heaven!" Dooley proclaimed when he spotted the next figure. "What's this? Tell me no one actually used such a mechanism!"

"Aye. This is the Judas Chair!" Tinsel whinnied.

A man was suspended from ropes on the ceiling. A metallic pyramid sat beneath him, its rusty tip penetrating the man's naked rear.

"Every day, the ropes were lowered . . . so the victim would be slowly sodomized by the chair! A terrible and protracted way to die! It was how homosexuals were punished in the old days."

"I'll have nightmares for weeks," Dooley said. "Better to kill 'em fast, I say! A mercy compared to this . . . this . . ."

"It's not called 'torture' for nothing, my good man!" Tinsel brayed.

"I think I'd rather leave this room."

"Sure. Sure. The next one is not quite so bloody, although it is disturbing."

The next room was easier, as promised. It portrayed creatures of myth and folklore. There was a hairy werewolf with a vulpine snout and black claws. It loomed over Dooley, its forelimbs stretched over its head. Dooley imagined one swipe from those claws would detach all the flesh from his bones as cleanly as a knife peels a fish.

Beside the wolf was a pair of witches. They were covered in boils, and they shared a singular eye between them. One witch was passing the eyeball to an expectant sister.

Tinsel told Dooley all he needed to know

at each creature. He informed him of the origins of their legends and which cultures still believed in them.

Dooley quite enjoyed the Gorgon, Medusa. She was a beautiful lady wearing a sheer nightgown. The only issue he had was that her hair was a bushel of wet, green snakes. Some of the snakes had open mouths, complete with needle-point fangs. Rather than look at the snakes, he stared happily at her curvy tits and dark nipples that glowed beneath the thin negligee.

"The next room is the newest exhibit," Tinsel informed his guest.

"I heard rumor, once, that you had a secret exhibit which only a special few have been allowed to see inside. Is that true?" Dooley inquired as they moved toward the next set of velvet curtains.

"Yes. But I've moved most of those artifacts into this room. And I've added some new ones," Tinsel said. "Come . . . come and have a look."

❄ ❄ ❄

Clovehitch followed Tinsel into the lobby. The old man was wearing his nightclothes, and his eyes were gummy with sleep.

"Drink, Constable? I assume you aren't on duty?"

"I'm not on duty at the second, no, but I'm not drinking with you. Not if what was said was true," Clovehitch grunted.

"Said by Dooley?"

"Yes." Clovehitch frowned. "He had quite a tale to tell. He spoke to us all at the pub. You're lucky I was there, or you'd have an angry mob to deal with rather than one irate constable."

"I thank you," Tinsel said. "So, you wanna look at the new exhibit? See if what Dooley saw was really there? See if I know all the details of . . . what happened?"

Clovehitch licked his chops. "Yes. That is what I'd like."

"Well, follow me then." Tinsel led the

way. "When he saw it, you know what he did, Constable?"

"He ran. He told me. He also told me he heard you laughing, even as he pounded his way through the door."

"Will you arrest me if what he said was true?"

"I'll bring you in for questioning," Clovehitch stated. "On suspicion of murder."

"Murder? My dear sir, my art only represents that which has already happened. I don't perpetrate it."

Clovehitch sniffed. "Art?"

"Yes. Whether you like it or not, I create art."

"When I think of art, I think of paintings of landscapes, and flowers, and fruit in bowls. Not . . . murder scenes."

"Just because you don't understand it—"

"Get on and show me this exhibit of yours."

"Are you sure you don't want to take your time? I have many models which could interest you—"

"I'm interested in the one that sent Dooley screaming down to the tavern. Show it to me."

"You were there, weren't you? You saw her—"

"Just show it to me." Clovehitch knocked Tinsel roughly on the shoulder.

Whimpering, the stooped man led him through the museum.

Clovehitch tried to ignore the other exhibits and models, but they caught his eye. Some looked as if they were leaping toward him, while others seemed as close to a real corpse as any he'd ever seen before.

When he got to the torture chamber, Clovehitch smelled the exact same scent of rotted meat Dooley had described.

"Christ. What is that?" Clovehitch swore.

Tinsel answered with a giggle. "I always keep a raw slab of steak and pork inside the interior of the Judas Chair here. I buy them at the market every month, set them outside so they fester for a few days, then bring them in and stow them away here. Adds to the atmosphere, don't it?"

"It certainly does!" Clovehitch rumbled. He wanted to vomit. "Let's move on!"

They came to the room of mythological beasts. The Gorgon was alluring, but Clovehitch laid eyes on another creature that caught his attention more than the shapely woman.

"What in God's name is *that*?"

"It's called Grindel. Have you ever read the epic of *Beowulf*?"

Clovehitch shook his head. "I don't know if I'd even want to read a book with something like that in it."

Grindel was tall, oafish, and toothy. He was human-formed, but his skin was lumpy and scaly, and he held a human head in his hands. Scraps of tattered flesh hung from his drooling mouth. His eyes were crazed, pointing in opposite directions.

"The next exhibit is the one that frightened poor Dooley. Are you prepared, Mr.

Clovehitch? I promise you, it lives up to expectations." Tinsel snickered.

Together, the two walked into the final section of the museum.

Clovehitch was confronted with it right away.

There she was, just as he'd seen her in the alleyway.

Molly was lying on the ground, spread-eagled, naked, and doused in frozen blood. Her organs were looped around her in a circle.

Clovehitch clenched his fists. He wished he was in uniform, just so he could use his baton to batter the deranged "artist" for his gratuity and tastelessness.

"You had no right to do this," Clovehitch declared with fervent fury.

"I do, though. It's a matter of public knowledge that Molly Dooley was murdered in the street. I was even able to access your statement for reference, Mr. Clovehitch. I wouldn't have known she'd been circled with her own intestines if not for you!"

"What were you thinking inviting Dooley to come and see this . . . this filth?"

"It's not filth, good sir. It's reality. You yourself considered realism to be art when you listed your examples. I model in realism too."

If Clovehitch was forced to compliment the man, it would only be to acknowledge that the model of Molly's demise was realistic. *Too realistic.*

He can't have gotten all this from a few reports and hearsay. This looks like something he'd actually seen. Or maybe . . . something he'd done!

"But this is only the start of the exhibit, Constable! Please, do not scurry off before you see the rest. I wonder . . . would Dooley have come to you if only he'd stuck around to see what other horrors I had to offer?"

Clovehitch felt his blood chill. "What's that supposed to mean, you daft prick?"

Tinsel snickered again. The noise was bothersome. It was like Tinsel was hiding a nasty piece of gossip but was ready to spill the beans at the first sign of prodding. "Look at the next exhibit, Mr. Clovehitch."

Clovehitch did.

His face went white.

He hadn't expected to see a wax model of himself. It was like looking into a mirror. A mirror into the past. A mirror of sins.

"H-how?" Clovehitch stammered.

Clovehitch always dressed like Father Christmas when he went hunting. The children trusted the jolly figure so much that they'd open their windows to allow him in without complaint. And all he had to do was press a white finger to his lips, and they'd be mouse-quiet until it was too late. Clovehitch hated it when his little darlings screamed, especially when their parents were just down the hall and could easily be awakened.

He'd knock on the hoarfrost-covered window and wait for the young babes to open up. When they did, their faces would be cherry red with delight. They'd step back and watch as he sidled into their rooms, his bag over his shoulder.

"Are you really him? Are you really—?"

"*Shhh*, my child!" Clovehitch would say, and the innocent one would zip their lips.

"You've been such a good boy this year, I decided to give you your present . . . personally!" Clovehitch would say. "Just close your eyes and keep very quiet. My Christmas magic doesn't work for naughty children . . . only good ones. And good children . . . don't . . . speak."

Clovehitch stared at the exhibit, his teeth chattering and his pupils expanding with fright and anger.

"Y-you can't show this to people," Clovehitch said.

"But, good sir . . . it's the truth," Tinsel mewled. "I only show the truth—"

Clovehitch spun. He landed a hard punch to Tinsel's mouth. The old man stumbled back, blurting with pain. Blood sputtered from his maw and repainted the floor.

Clovehitch grabbed him by the scruff of his neck and hauled him close.

"You can't do this to me!"

"You're . . . the monster . . . Clovehitch. Not me. YOU!" Tinsel released a guttural blast of blood, staining the constable's face.

Clovehitch swung a fist. The punch landed against Tinsel's skull, knocking his head to the side. He released the old man just as he pounded him, sending him sprawling.

Tinsel hit the ground, lying right beside Molly's corpse.

"You can't do this to me!" Clovehitch stamped over and stomped on Tinsel's weak stomach. The old man sputtered and brayed, launching another gob of blood into the air. "I'm an important member of Downwhich, you bastard! It's my word against yours! It's *my* word against *yours*! And I'm going to burn your putrid museum to the ground! Do you hear me? None of those brats talked because they knew. They knew they had no chance of stopping me!"

Clovehitch knelt down and put his hands around Tinsel's neck. He squeezed, and the old man began to gibber with panic.

"I'm good all year! I only do it at Christmas! It's my gift to myself, you . . . you puke! You sham! I'm not *a monster!*"

Tinsel smiled. It was bloodred. "They talked, you animal! They . . . talked!"

Clovehitch's face fell. He alleviated his hold on Tinsel's neck.

"H-how did you know?"

"Because they told me . . . what you do . . . that you choose one every Christmas. They told me . . . and that's why . . . that's why . . . I made it."

Clovehitch scowled. "Then I'll take care of them after I'm done with you."

Clovehitch heard a *click*.

He looked up.

Dooley was standing at the threshold, holding his double-barreled shotgun.

"Dooley!" Clovehitch scrambled.

"Goodbye, Constable."

Dooley pulled the trigger.

Clovehitch's scream was cut short when a blast of hot fire punched through his face. Gray brains spilled from the back of his head and carpeted the floor behind him. He threw his arms into the air and jumped up and back. When he landed, he skidded in his own gore, then lay still.

Dooley stepped into the room and lowered his weapon. He looked toward Tinsel.

"Are you okay?"

Tinsel rubbed his neck. "I didn't know this plan of yours would work. I'm glad it did. The bastard," he growled.

"Sorry it took me so long to get here. I had to explain the true story to the patrons at the bar. Let them know why I'd really come in. I don't know if they all believe it. They're waiting outside now. I must admit, I painted quite a ghoulish image of you when I first told the tale. I made it seem you'd surprised me with this . . . just like we planned. They fell for every word."

"Hopefully, my reputation hasn't been totally ruined," Tinsel rubbed his bruised face. "Or, ruined any more than it already was."

Dooley looked at Molly's body. "I don't know who killed her. Whether Clovehitch had any part in it or not. But when those children told me at Sunday school what Clovehitch had done to them and why they dreaded Christmas, I couldn't help but think of my Molly. How if I knew who'd done it . . . I would want the prick eliminated from the world."

He helped Tinsel to his feet. Side-by-side, the two walked away from the abominable wax project they'd designed together.

More publications by Judith Sonnet:

Low Blasphemy

The Shriek-A-Rama Spook Show Experience

Torture the Sinners!

The Clown Hunt

Magick

No One Rides For Free

Beast of Burden

Psych Ward Blues

Blood and Brains

Hot Musket

Every Night in the Bone Orchard

The Home (Coming January 15th)

Anthologies curated by Judith Sonnet:

Scraps: A Splatterpunk Anthology

Gasps: A Quiet Horror Anthology

Screams: A Horror Anthology